The Bombed House

Jonny Zucker

Illustrated by
Paul Savage

FULL FLIGHT

Titles in Full Flight 2

The Bombed House	Jonny Zucker
Gang of Fire	Jonny Zucker
Big Brother @ School	Jillian Powell
Rollercoaster	Jillian Powell
Monster Planet	David Orme
Danger Mountain	David Orme
Goal Scorers	Jonny Zucker
Basketball	Tony Norman
Fight to the Death! A play	Stan Cullimore
Stop Talking at the Back and other poems	(ed.) Jonny Zucker

Badger Publishing Limited
26 Wedgwood Way, Pin Green Industrial Estate, Stevenage,
Hertfordshire SG1 4QF
Telephone: 01438 356907. Fax: 01438 747015.
www.badger-publishing.co.uk   enquiries@badger-publishing.co.uk

The Bombed House ISBN 1 85880 369 1

Series Editor: Jonny Zucker
Publisher: David Jamieson
Editor: Paul Martin
Design: Jain Birchenough
Cover illustration: Paul Savage
Printed and bound in China through Colorcraft Ltd., Hong Kong

The Bombed House

Jonny Zucker

Contents

Badger Publishing

Chapter 1 - Number 46

January 1941. The middle of the Blitz. German planes had been bombing London for weeks.

Ned and Harry Jennings were running down Willow Street kicking a football. Their house, number 27, was OK but many of the houses on the street had been smashed to bits.

Most of their friends had been evacuated to families in the country, but some hadn't been so lucky.

Like their best mate Charlie Smith from number 33. He had died three months ago, along with all of his family when a German bomb hit their house.

A family hadn't been found yet for Ned and Harry, so they were still in London.

Waiting.

They stopped outside number 46 Willow Street.

The top half of the house had been blasted off, so it just stood there.

Half a house.

The owners, Mr and Mrs Young, were safe. They were staying down on the coast with friends.

Harry bent down to look in the rubble lying in the street, but Ned walked a bit closer to the house.

He was looking in one of the windows when he heard a noise coming from inside. It sounded like a groan.

"Harry" he called. "I heard a noise in there."

Harry stood up and looked at him.

"Don't be stupid Ned," he answered, checking his watch, "there's nothing there, and anyway we need to get home."

They started to walk back towards their house.

Ned looked back at number 46.

He knew he wasn't wrong.

Chapter 2 - The Put Down

The next day, Ned told Harry he was going to say something about number 46 to their dad. Mr Jennings was a member of the Home Guard, in charge of safety on Willow Street.

"I'll mention it at supper."

"Don't bother," said Harry, "you're making a fuss out of nothing."

But Harry did talk about it that evening.

Their dad smiled and tapped his fingers on the kitchen table after Ned had told him.

"Listen Ned," he began, "I know you mean well but there are far more important things happening at the moment than your adventure games.

"There are German bombers flying over London every day - one plane was shot down last week only about a mile away from here."

"But dad I did hear something," claimed Ned.

Mrs Jennings held up her hand.

"Maybe he's right Bill," she said softly, "maybe the Home Guard should have a look round number 46."

"Alright, alright" replied Mr Jennings, "I'll get some of the ladj11 s to check it out, but I don't want you two going anywhere near that house. It's a death trap. Do you hear me?"

They both nodded.

"Right," said Mr Jennings, "now can we get on with eating our supper?"

But the booming noise of the air-raid siren sounded and they all stood up at once.

"Don't forget your gas masks boys," called Mrs Jennings.

The four of them ran out of the house
and down the street to the air-raid
shelter on the corner.

Chapter 3 - Face at the Window

On Saturday, Ned and Harry went to their Aunt Rose's for tea.

Rose told great stories about her childhood in Scotland and she made good use of her rations to bake superb cakes.

They left her house as it was getting dark and walked home quickly.

As they were passing number 46 Willow Street, they both looked at its gloomy front.

Then, from inside the house, a pale face appeared at one of the windows.

It was there for a split second, and then it vanished.

But they both saw it.

"Oh my god Ned, you were right!" hissed Harry, "there's someone in there. We've got to find out who it is."

Slowly, they crept up to the front door and Harry leaned forward to push it open.

They walked inside the dark hallway.

They'd only taken a few steps when part of the roof started to cave in. Rubble came crashing down at great speed.

They turned back and fled from the house, watching as more rubble tumbled down.

"We were lucky not to be buried alive," said Ned.

They ran home and burst through the front door. Their mum and dad were in the kitchen having a cup of tea.

"We saw a face at the window of number 46!" shouted Harry.

"And we went inside to look, but part of the roof fell in," added Ned.

"You did what?" demanded their father. He looked very angry. "You could have got yourselves killed," he barked at them. "I told you to stay away!"

"But we saw someone. We both did!" insisted Ned.

"Stop this nonsense!" commanded Mr Jennings. "For your information, I got two of the Home Guard lads to have a look round in there this afternoon. They found nothing at all. Did you hear me? Nothing."

"But dad..." mouthed Ned.

"But dad nothing," replied Mr Jennings. "Number 46 is totally out of bounds to both of you. The matter is closed and that's final."

Chapter 4 - Follow Danger

Ned and Harry sat in their bedroom.
They were sure they had seen a face at
the window, but their dad just hadn't
wanted to listen. And the Home Guard
had checked out the place.

Their mum knocked on the door and
came in.

She sat down on Harry's bed with
them.

"Look boys," she started, "dad's not
really angry with you. He just doesn't
want you getting into any sort of
danger. We know you want to help out,
but it's very easy to imagine things in
the middle of a war."

Ned was about to say something, but
Harry shook his head.

Ned said nothing.

Their mum talked with them for a few
more minutes and then left the room.

"I'm sorry I didn't believe you at first," said Harry.

"It's OK, don't worry," replied Ned.

"There's something weird going on at number 46," Harry mouthed quietly.

"But dad said stay away from it," said Ned.

"It doesn't matter what dad said," whispered Harry. "Danger of death or not, we're going in there to find out what's going on."

Chapter 5 - Night Moves

Early the next morning there was a knock on their front door.

It was a woman with some papers. She sat in the kitchen with Mr and Mrs Jennings.

Ned and Harry walked in.

"What's going on?" asked Ned.

"This is Mrs Thornton," their mum explained. "They've found a family for you in the Lake District. Mrs Thornton has got all of the paperwork for your evacuation. The family you're going to are called the Robinsons. You'll be leaving for them tomorrow morning."

Ned flashed a look at Harry.

The whole of that day, their dad
watched them like a hawk.

"I only want you in the back yard or
inside," he said.

As soon as it got dark, he told them to
get ready for bed.

Ned started to complain but
Mr Jennings wasn't having it.

"You've got an early start in the
morning. I've got a Home Guard shift
tonight," he said sternly, "and I don't
want you giving your mum any
trouble."

They went up to their bedroom and sat quietly.

Twenty minutes later they heard their dad saying goodbye to their mum and leaving the house.

Mrs Jennings turned on the wireless in the kitchen. The boys could hear the low drone of a war report.

They turned off their bedroom light and waited for half an hour. Then Harry carefully slid open their bedroom window. He looked at Ned.

Ned nodded.

As quietly as they could, they climbed out of the window, shinned down the drainpipe and onto the ground at the front of their house.

The noise of the wireless hummed from the kitchen.

They looked around them in the darkness. There was no one to be seen.

They stepped out onto the street.

Chapter 6 - In Like a Shot

Willow Street was completely dark because of the black out.

After a few minutes their eyes got used to the darkness and they found number 46.

Creeping silently, they stepped over the rubble and inside the house.

The hallway was covered with fallen bricks and pieces of broken wood.

Harry pulled a flash light out of his pocket and turned it on.

They walked into the kitchen. Harry shone the light. Nothing to be seen.

They looked in the sitting-room.
Nothing.

The bathroom. Nothing.

"Maybe dad was right after all,"
muttered Ned.

It was then that Harry shone his light
down the steps that led to the cellar.

As he moved the beam from left to right, something suddenly glinted in its light. It was a black cross.

"Did you see that?" whispered Harry.

Without warning, the sound of a gunshot suddenly filled the air and a bullet went whizzing past them.

Seconds later another gunshot sounded and Ned felt an incredible jab of pain in his left arm.

He stumbled and fell forward down the cellar steps.

Harry called out and jumped down after him.

Chapter 7 - The Return

There were voices everywhere.
One of the voices was their dad's.

He and other members of the Home
Guard piled into the house and down
the cellar steps.

Ned had been shot in the arm and had fallen into a German soldier.

Harry was holding the soldier's gun with all of his strength.

The Home Guards leapt onto the soldier and held him down.

The soldier screamed at them in German.

Mr Jennings and some of the other Home Guards held a whispered conversation, and then the German soldier was dragged away, kicking and yelling.

Mr Jennings shone a torch onto Ned's arm.

"You're very lucky," he said quietly. "It's not too bad, but we'll need to get you to a hospital tonight. We'll go home first quickly and tell your mum what's going on."

The three of them walked up the cellar steps and out of the house into the pitch-black street.

"You've just given me the fright of my life," said Mr Jennings slowly, "and I know you disobeyed me, but I'm really proud of you."

"I'm sorry for not listening to you properly," he added. "Two lads from the Home Guard checked out the house, but they did it very quickly and they clearly didn't search the cellar.

"It's my fault, I told them just to have a quick look."

"What were you whispering to those other Home Guards about?" asked Harry.

"We were talking about the German," explained Mr Jennings. "We reckon he's the pilot of the plane that was shot down last week. He must have found his way to number 46 and been hiding out there."

"What will they do with him?" asked Harry.

"He'll be handed over to the army and become a prisoner of war," replied Mr Jennings.

"Do you think we'll still be going to the Lake District tomorrow?" asked Ned.

"If the hospital gives you the all clear, son, you'll both be on that train in the morning."

They reached their house.

Mrs Jennings was standing on the doorstep looking frantic with worry.

"I heard gun shots," she whispered. "What's going on Bill? And what are you two doing out in the street?"

"It's nothing to worry about," Mr Jennings replied. "Ned and Harry just need to get their coats for the walk to hospital."

"Hospital?" asked Mrs Jennings, with fear in her voice.

"It's Ned's arm," explained Mr Jennings, putting his arm round his wife's shoulders. "I'll explain it all to you on the way there. He'll be completely fine."

Their dad gazed up into the night sky and saw their bedroom window.

It was wide open.

He looked slowly from the window to his sons.

"Next time, use the front door," he smiled.